MARCO
GOES TO SCHOOL

Roz Chast

atheneum books for young readers

new york   london   toronto   sydney   new delhi

ATHENEUM BOOKS FOR YOUNG READERS

An imprint of Simon & Schuster Children's Publishing Division

1230 Avenue of the Americas, New York, New York 10020

ATHENEUM BOOKS FOR YOUNG READERS is a registered trademark of Simon & Schuster, Inc.

For information about special discounts for bulk purchases, please contact

Simon & Schuster Special Sales at 1-866-506-1949 or business@simonandschuster.com.

The Simon & Schuster Speakers Bureau can bring authors to your live event.

For more information or to book an event, contact the Simon & Schuster Speakers Bureau

at 1-866-248-3049 or visit our website at www.simonspeakers.com.

Book design by Lizzy Bromley.

The text for this book is set in Edlund.

The illustrations for this book are rendered in watercolor.

Manufactured in China

0512 SCP

First Edition

2 4 6 8 10 9 7 5 3 1

Library of Congress Cataloging-in-Publication Data

Chast, Roz.

Marco goes to school / written and illustrated by Roz Chast. — 1st ed.

p. cm.

Summary: Marco the bird is eager to start school because he wants to learn how to reach the moon, and
although he does not accomplish that on his first day, he does make a new friend.

ISBN 978-1-4169-8475-7 (hardcover : alk. paper)

ISBN 978-1-4424-5307-4 (eBook)

[1. Birds—Fiction. 2. First day of school—Fiction. 3. Schools—Fiction. 4. Friendship—Fiction. 5. Humorous
stories.] I. Title.

PZ7.C3877Mar 2012

[E]—dc22

2011002565

To my nonfeathery children,
Ian and Nina

Marco was BORED!

Watching TV
was boring.

Playing in his sandbox
was boring.

Helping his mom fold laundry
was boring.

He'd been really good about
cleaning his room lately.
Surely that would be
worth one new toy.

He was just about to point out that
fact to his mom when she walked in.

"No," said his mom. "School is a place for kids your age, where they go to learn things."

Like WHAT? thought Marco. He already knew a lot of things, like what the best lunch in the world was, which was why he had it every day.

Finally the big day arrived.
Marco and his mom drove to school.
His head was chirping with questions.

He also wondered who might be in his class.

His mom dropped him off at the school yard and kissed him good-bye.
While he was waiting for this "school" thing to start, he . . .

hula-hooped with someone's lost hair tie . . .

chewed on a blade of grass . . .

got his shoe stuck in a wad of gum . . .

kicked a marble around and . . .   folded a gum wrapper into a hat.

He was starting to feel a little lonely.

But Marco wasn't alone for long!

The lady with the flowered pants was Mrs. Peachtree, their teacher.

Mrs. Peachtree seemed nice, and her pants were definitely interesting.
But then Marco saw something REALLY interesting.

During Mrs. Peachtree's next lesson, Marco's thoughts were far, far away.

BUT HOW WAS HE SUPPOSED TO GET TO THE MOON?

Marco was glad HIS mom knew how to pack a lunch.

Mary had a sardine-and-chocolate sandwich.

BLECH!

Jessica had four slices of bologna and a little bag of crackers.

EWW!

And poor Henry! He had a box of frozen peas!

PEAS

GROSS!

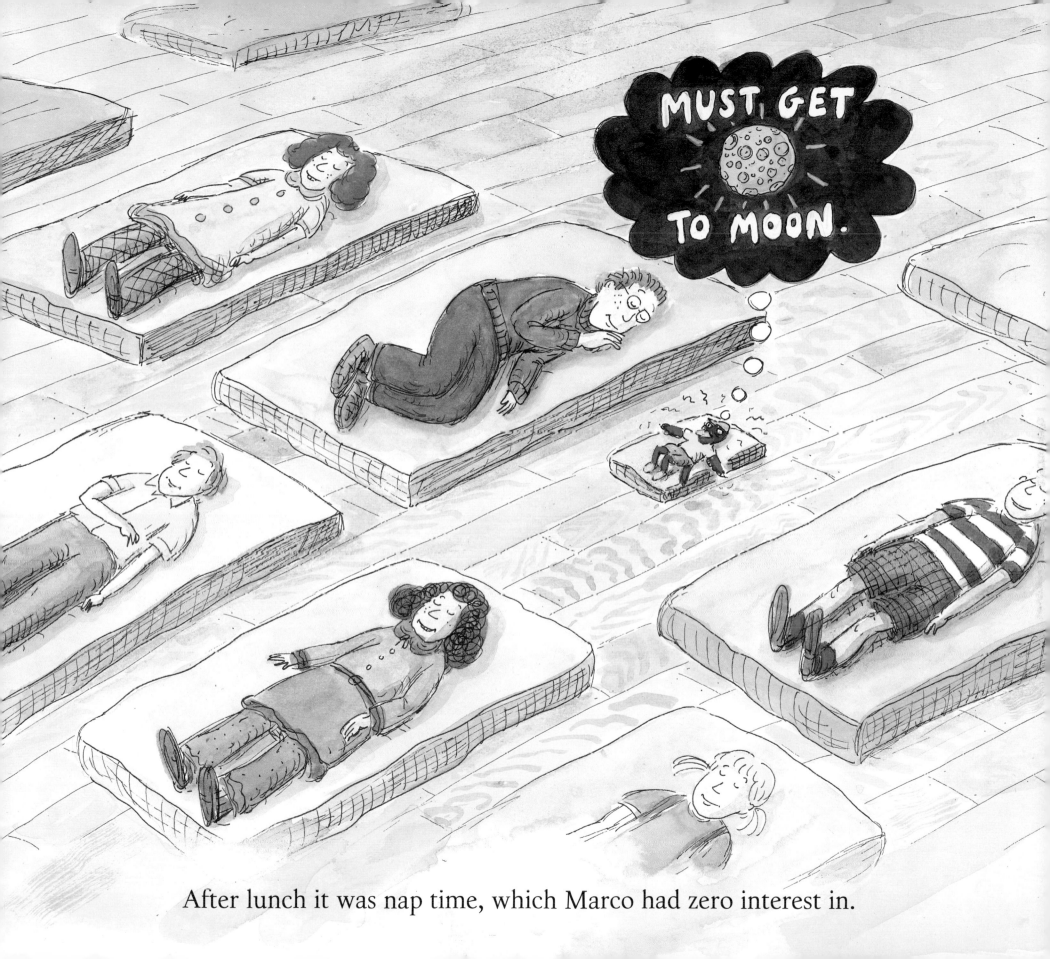

After lunch it was nap time, which Marco had zero interest in.

Finally it was playtime, but Marco
knew it was time to get to work.

Everyone pitched in. After all, who wouldn't want to go to the moon?

the whole plan came crashing down. Blocks were everywhere.
Marco was just a small bird with a big dream.

Just then Mrs. Peachtree came up with a plan of her own.

All you had to do was aim the blocks into the Blocks Box.
Henry and Marco worked as a team, because Marco was
a little bit on the short side.

No one made it to the moon that day,
but Marco did make a friend.